Tessa the Teacher

Felicity Brooks

Illustrated by Jo Litchfield

Designed by Nickey Butler

Educational consultant: Moira Taplin

Cover design by Amanda Gulliver

It's early in the morning and Tessa the Teacher (Miss Thompson to the children) is racing down the hill to school. She has to get there before the children arrive.

"Good morning," says Mr. Goransky the caretaker. "You're early today."

Here's what Tessa has in her work bag.

Keys for her classroom and bike lock

Pens for marking

Food for lunch

Notebooks for lesson plans, and some letters

This board shows some of the people Tessa works with.

Mr. Mason is Tessa's friend.

Some children find
Mrs. McGregor a little scary!

Mrs. Harrison

Headteacher

Mr. Mason

Music teacher

Miss Singh

Infant teacher

Mrs. McGregor

Class teacher

Littletown School

Mr. Goransky

School
caretaker

Mrs. Butler

Classroom
assistant

Mrs. Chen

School secretary

Miss Thompson

Class teacher

Mrs. Butler helps Tessa
in her classroom.

Tessa says hello to Mrs. Butler. "Are you ready for our play today?" she asks.
"I think so," says Mrs. Butler. "I just hope the children are!"

Soon the children start to arrive. They are very excited.

Olivia   Bijal   Leon   Amber   Anna

"I like your hairband."

"I've got new shoes."

Miss Thompson's Class

Carlos · Jonathan · Alfred · Laura · Georgia · Olivia · Leon · Bijal · Carla · Ben · Robert · Sarah · Jose · Paula · Amir · Lia · Amber · Seth · Meena · Anna · Eva · Joshua

"Has anyone seen Joshua?"

arla · Seth · Georgia · Eva · Joshua

"Where's my pink pencil?"

"My sister's got chicken pops."

5

When Tessa raises her hand, the children know they have to sit down quietly.

"Now – sit down please, Joshua!" says Tessa. "I hope everyone's here as we're doing our 'Clever Crocodile' play this afternoon."

"My dad's coming!"

"My auntie's coming too!"

Tessa calls out the names on the register and waits for each child to answer.

Tessa writes an "A" for children who are away. Can you see who's away today?

	Monday				
Jose Alvarez	A	✓	✓	✓	
Carla Armstrong		✓	✓	✓	✓
Meena Bhatti		✓	✓	✓	A
Amber Brennan		✓	✓	✓	✓
Paula Cannon		✓	✓	✓	✓
Bijal Chakrabarti		✓	✓	✓	✓
Alfred Chung	A	✓	✓	✓	
Lia Cox		✓	✓	✓	✓
Leon Fernandez		✓	✓	✓	✓
Joshua Firth		✓	✓	✓	✓
Ben Flowers		✓	✓	✓	✓
Carlos Garcia		✓	A	✓	✓
Amir Iqbal		✓	✓	A	✓
Georgia Johnson		✓	✓	✓	✓
Seth Larkin		✓	✓	✓	✓
Anna Lim		✓	✓	✓	✓
Robert Owen		✓	✓	✓	A
Laura Munro		✓	✓	✓	✓
Jonathan Turner		✓	✓	✓	✓
Olivia Sims		✓	✓	✓	✓
Sarah Stratton		✓			
Eva Waters					

Suddenly the door bursts open. Paula Cannon rushes in.

"Hello," says Tessa. "What happened to you?"

"Sorry," pants Paula. "My sister threw her hippo out of her buggy and we had to go back to look for it."

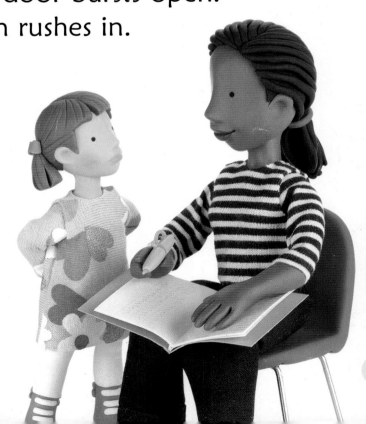

Then Mrs. Chen is at the door.
"Jonathan's mum called," she says.
"He has a tummy bug."

"Oh no!" says Tessa. "Poor Jon.
He's supposed to be the clever crocodile."

"Could you be the croc?" Tessa
asks Carlos while the class work.
"I know all the words," he says.
"Great!" says Tessa. "We'll
practise later."

Tessa looks at the children's news books.

Dad spilled some paint all over the floor.

My mum has a new green dress and a lovely red bag.

Georgia came to my house and we played with our new kitten.

Georgia

kitten

me

Next, they share a story about a big red tractor.

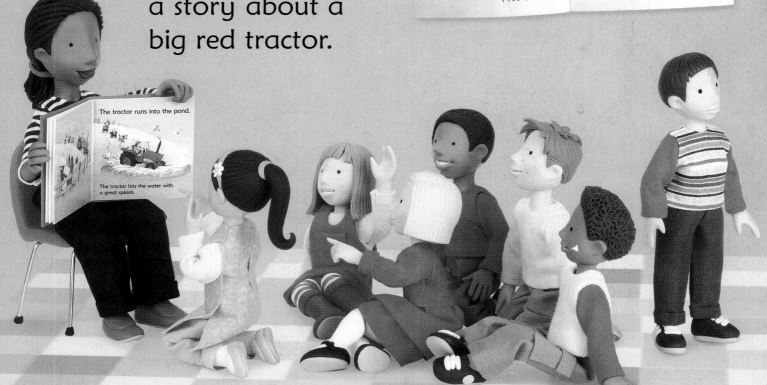

The tractor runs into the pond.

The tractor hits the water with a great splash.

At playtime, Tessa works outside.
Lots of the children need her help.

Carla grazes
her knee.

Robert loses
his snack.

Sarah and
Laura have
an argument.

Amir can't
find his shoes.

10

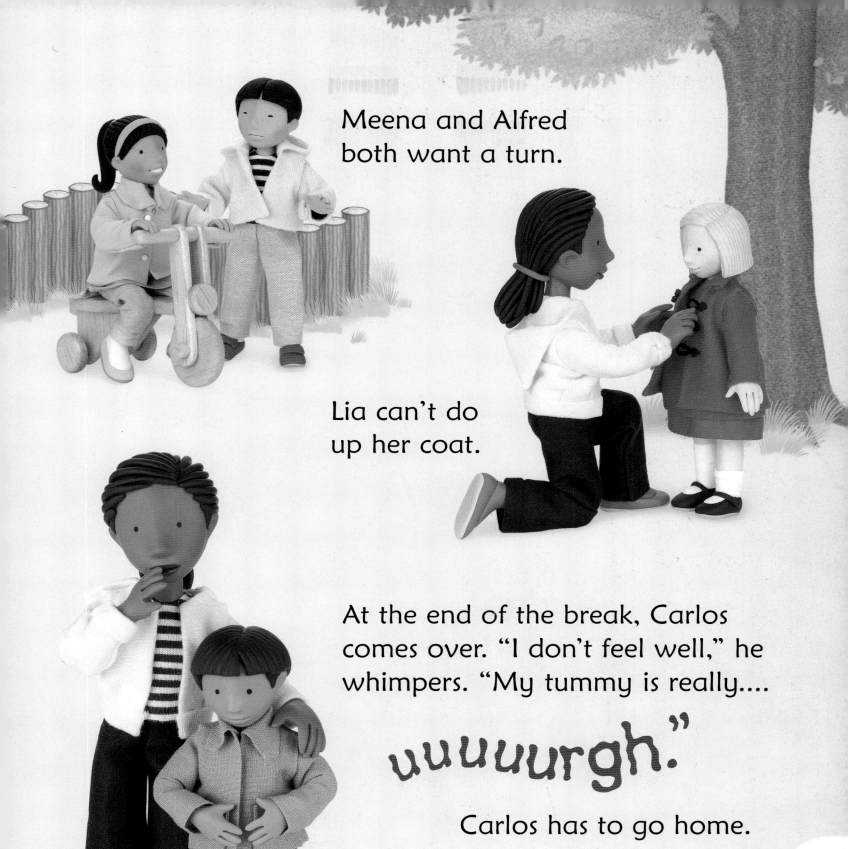

Meena and Alfred
both want a turn.

Lia can't do
up her coat.

At the end of the break, Carlos
comes over. "I don't feel well," he
whimpers. "My tummy is really....

uuuuurgh."

Carlos has to go home.

After playtime, Tessa explains that there's no one to play the crocodile again.

"Lia should do it," suggests Anna. "She can sing really well."

"Would you like to try?" Tessa asks.
"Errrr... OK," says Lia.
"Good! We'll practise after lunch –
sit down please, Joshua!"

The children finish their
costumes and posters
for the play.

Lia tries on the crocodile mask.
"You look like a very clever crocodile," says Tessa.

"OwWW," says a voice inside the mask.
"My tummy hurts."

"Oh no," says Tessa.
"Not another sick croc!"

"My crocs keep getting sick," Tessa tells Mr. Mason at lunchtime. "It's too late to cancel. What can I do?"

"We're all looking forward to your play this afternoon," chips in Mrs. Harrison.

"Hmmm... so am I," says Tessa, trying to smile.

After lunch, it's time to practice the play, but no one wants to be the crocodile.

"Too sc-a-a-a-ry," says Meena.

"Too **big**," says Joshua.

"Too small," says Seth.

"Too **heavy**," says Olivia.

"Too soon," says Bijal.

"Too late," says Tessa. "I'll just have to say the crocodile's words myself."

People start to arrive to see the play.

"Now – sit down please, Joshua!" says Tessa.
"I'll tell the audience we have no crocodile today,
and then we'll begin. Is everyone ready?"

"It'll be really
bad without a
proper crocodile."

"I know,
and my auntie's
watching. It's soooo
embarrassing."

Mr. Mason plays the piano to begin the play. The audience goes quiet.

Tessa takes a deep breath and is about to step out into the hall...

Just then someone runs up behind her. Tessa spins around.

"Jonathan!" she cries.
"I'm feeling much better," says Jon.
"Quick! On with your costume," says Tessa. "It's time to start."

The play goes well. Nearly everyone remembers what to do and Jon sings the crocodile song beautifully.

"Snap, snap go my teeth in the river.
Snap, snap go my teeth in the mud..."

"So the clever crocodile found he had lots of friends and was never, ever lonely again."

The class take a bow.

Tessa is really proud of them.

"Stand up, Joshua!"

"HURRAH!"

"Let's give Miss Thompson and Mrs. Butler a big clap," says Mrs. Harrison.

After the play, Tessa talks to some parents and teachers.

"Didn't they do a fantastic job?"

"Well done, Miss Thompson!"

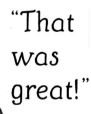

"That was great!"

Back in the classroom, Tessa says thank you and goodbye to the children.

While she's tidying up, Mrs. Harrison comes in.

"Don't forget the staff meeting today," she says to Tessa. "We must talk about the school concert. Would you like to organize it this year?"

"Just as long as there's no crocodile in it!" laughs Tessa.

Class photo quiz

Littletown School

Miss Thompson's Class

Amir Iqbal, Laura Munro, Seth Larkin, Bijal Chakrabarti

Miss Thompson, Jonathan Turner, Alfred Chung, Lia Cox, Jose Alvarez, Meena Bhatti, Mrs. Butler

Olivia Sims, Carlos Garcia, Paula Cannon, Anna Lim, Sarah Stratton, Leon Fernandez

Carla Armstrong, Robert Owen, Eva Waters, Georgia Johnson, Joshua Firth, Ben Flowers, Amber Brennan

Here's a photo of Tessa and her class.
Look back and see if you can find
all these children in the book.

Photography: MMStudios

With thanks to Staedtler UK for providing the Fimo® material for models;
Abbie Hayward for paintings on pages 3 and 21; Olivia Brooks for illustrations on page 9;
Mrs. J Clerke and the pupils and staff at Melbourne Infant school, Derbyshire, UK;
Mrs. van den Eshof and her class, Charlbury Primary School, Oxfordshire, UK, and
Libby Thrumbull and her class, Thousand Oaks Elementary School, Berkeley, California, USA.

www.usborne.com
First published in 2006 by Usborne Publishing Ltd.,
Usborne House, 83-85 Saffron Hill, London EC1N 8RT, England. Copyright ©2006 Usborne Publishing Ltd.